Size

Written by Felicia Law
Illustrated by Paula Knight

NORWOODHOUSE PRESS

Chicago, Illinois

DEAR CAREGIVER The **Patchwork** series is a whimsical collection of books that integrate poetry to reinforce primary concepts among emergent readers. You might consider these modern-day nursery rhymes that are relevant for today's children. For example, rather than a Miss Muffet sitting on a tuffet, eating her curds and whey, your child will encounter a Grandma and Grandpa dancing a Samba, or a big sister who knows how to make rocks skim and the best places to swim.

Not only do the poetry and prose within the **Patchwork** books help children broaden their understanding of the concepts and recognize key words, the rhyming text helps them develop phonological awareness—an underlying skill necessary for success in transitioning from emergent to conventional readers.

As you read the text, invite your child to help identify the words that rhyme, start and end with similar sounds, or find the words connected to the pictures. The pictures in these books feature illustrations resembling the technique of torn-paper collage. The artwork can inspire young artists to experiment with torn-paper to create images and write their own poetry.

Above all, the most important part of the reading experience is to have fun and enjoy it!

Sincerely,

Shannon Cannon

Shannon Cannon, Ph.D.
Literacy Consultant

Norwood House Press • P.O. Box 316598 • Chicago, Illinois 60631
For more information about Norwood House Press please visit our website at
www.norwoodhousepress.com or call 866-565-2900.

LIBRARY OF CONGRESS CATALOGING-IN-PUBLICATION DATA
Law, Felicia.
  Size / by Felicia Law ; illustrated by Paula Knight.
     pages cm. -- (Patchwork)
  Summary: Torn paper collages and simple, rhyming text portray people encountering objects of many different sizes, from big and little cars to children of nearly the same height. Includes a word list.
  ISBN 978-1-59953-713-9 (library edition : alk. paper) -- ISBN 978-1-60357-811-0 (ebook)
[1. Stories in rhyme. 2. Size--Fiction.] I. Knight, Paula, illustrator. II. Title.
  PZ8.3.L3544Siz 2015
  [E]--dc23
                                        2014047194

274N—062015
Manufactured in the United States of America in North Mankato, Minnesota.

Huge elephant

You're bigger than a house

Bigger than a bus

Bigger than my Dad's van

You're e-nor-mous

Wider than a billboard

Taller than a tree

Bigger than just about everything

and that includes me!

3

All sorts

Big and little
Fat and thin
Saggy
Baggy
All tucked in
Hefty
Tiny
Tall and wide
Long and narrow

Every size

Big, Small

Vroom vroom, spinning wheels

Engine roars, brake squeals

Vroom vroom, along the grass

Watch out people – let me pass

Shoosh whoosh, cruise control

Silent engine, wheels roll

Shoosh whoosh, along the street

Waving to the folks I meet

7

Socks

Toe slippers

Ankle dippers

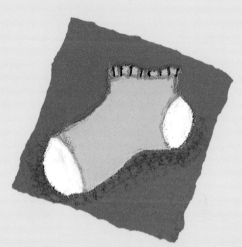

Half-leg huggers

Knee snuggers

Heel corners

Foot warmers

9

Tall flower

The seed I planted
In the ground
Has grown with sun and water

It's now a flower
So strong and tall
It makes me look much shorter

Little bug

Tiny little ladybug
   Small from head to tail
Smaller than my finger
   Rounder than my nail

You don't nod or smile at me
   You don't say 'Good day'
You walk up and down a bit
   And then you fly away

13

Big sister

My big sister knows exactly what to do
She knows where sweet berries grow
And which nuts are good to chew
She finds the easy trees to climb
And the lost path through the wood
She lets me into her secret den
When I promise to be good
She stands on the riverbank
Throwing stones to make them skim
She knows where it is shallow
And the best places to swim

Growing in and out

Last year

This hat, this vest, these shoes

Were my best set

❀

Next year

This top, these pants

Will fit, I bet

17

18

My two cats

Plump and fluffy
Sloppy Milly
White and puffy
Really silly!

Thin and scrawny
Scratchy and cross
Grey and lean
But Dan's the boss!

19

Growing together

I'm taller - says Lucy
You're not - says Flo
And I bet I'll keep up
As fast as you grow

I'm winning - says Lucy
No you're up on your toes
And I'm level - says Flo
In line with your nose

21

This book includes these concept words:

- big
- cat
- climb
- elephant
- fast
- fat
- flower
- fluffy
- good
- ground
- grow
- half

house	nose	thin
huge	plump	tiny
ladybug	sock	water
little	street	wide
long	strong	wood
narrow	tall	year